The Half-Term Rabbit

Written and illustrated by
Thelma Lambert

Hamish Hamilton
London

First published in Great Britain 1985
by Hamish Hamilton Children's Books
Garden House 57–59 Long Acre London WC2E 9JZ
Text copyright © 1985 by Thelma Lambert
Illustrations copyright © 1985 by Thelma Lambert

For Ben Hsiung

British Library Cataloguing in Publication Data
Lambert, Thelma
The Half-term Rabbit.——(Cartwheels)
I. Title   II. Series
823'.914[J]   PZ7

ISBN 0–241–11598–1

Colour separations by Anglia Reproductions
Typeset by Katerprint Co. Ltd, Oxford
Printed in Great Britain by
Blantyre Printing and Binding Ltd
London and Glasgow

It was half-term.

Everyone in Class One was busy tidying up.

Then Miss Bell called for silence.

"Now, who is going to look after Snowy over the half-term?"

Snowy was the Class pet, a big fluffy white rabbit.

"Nicky was going to take him, Miss,
but she's away with the mumps!" said
Jill. Miss Bell looked worried.

"Oh dear," she said. "What shall I do
with Snowy?"

"I'll take him," said Benny, the
smallest boy in the class. "My Dad likes
animals."

When school was over, Benny waited in the playground with the rabbit in its wooden hutch. One by one all the children and all the teachers went home. Only Benny and Snowy were left.

Benny began to feel lonely. Had Dad forgotten him?

Just then his big brother Tom came
running up the path.

"What have you got there?" he asked.

"It's Snowy. No one could look after
him for the half-term, so I said we
would take him . . ."

Tom made a face.

"Dad has got enough to do without a rabbit to look after as well," Tom said.

Benny felt sad. He looked down at Snowy, who was nibbling a carrot.

Then Benny smiled.

"I know! I'll hide him in the garden shed and look after him myself. Dad won't even know. Snowy can be our secret. Please, Tom!"

"Oh, all right then," said Tom.

Benny looked after Snowy all by
himself. He took carrots out to him.
He gave him water each day. And
no one except Tom knew he was there.

"Funny!" said Dad when he was cooking one day. "I thought I had lots of carrots for the stew. There are none left . . ."

Dad was surprised when Benny said he would go down to the shop to get some more.

The next day Benny's little sister,
Becky, went out to play in the garden.
Tom had gone out with his friends.

Dad was busy making a cake for Benny's
birthday, and Benny was helping.

Suddenly Becky came running in from
the garden.

"I've been playing with a big white
rabbit," she said. "But now he's run
away. I want him back!" she wailed.

Dad smiled. "A big white rabbit?"
he said. "That's a good story, Becky!"

14

Benny dropped his mixing-spoon and rushed out to the shed. The rabbit-hutch door was wide open — and Snowy had gone! The rabbit was nowhere to be seen. Benny looked in the bushes and behind the trees.

He began to feel afraid.

What if he had lost the Class rabbit? What would Miss Bell say?

Then Benny peeped through a hole in
the fence into Old Grumpy's garden.
There was Snowy!

He was eating the cabbages! But Benny
didn't dare go into Mrs Watson's garden
to try and get Snowy back.

Mrs Watson was not called "Old Grumpy" for nothing. She often waved her stick at the children and shouted after them.

Benny was sure she was a witch. She even had a black cat . . .

Just then the black cat saw Snowy and began to run after him.

Benny squeezed through a gap in the fence and joined in the chase. But Snowy was too quick. He ran all around Old Grumpy's garden and then ran back into Benny's garden and straight into the kitchen.

Dad was just lifting the cake into the
tin when Snowy dashed by, like a flash of
white lightning.

"What on earth . . ." Dad was so
surprised that he dropped the cake onto
the kitchen floor.

"My cake!" Dad cried.

Benny tried to catch the rabbit but
Snowy was too quick for him.

"Mind the cake on the floor, Benny!"
cried Dad.

But Dad's warning came too late.
Benny fell right on top of his lovely, iced
birthday cake.

At last Snowy stopped for a rest under the kitchen table. Dad quickly picked up the frightened rabbit and stroked him.

After Benny had cleaned himself up, he told Dad the whole story.

Dad marched out to the shed, with
Snowy in his arms.

"Look — his drinking water has
turned into ice," said Dad. "It's too cold
out here for him. Let's bring him into
the kitchen — but you'll have to clean
out the hutch first."

"Yes, Dad!" said Benny. "Thanks for
letting me keep him."

Benny felt very happy.

"But I'm afraid you won't have a
birthday cake now," said Dad. "It's
completely ruined . . ."

23

Benny stopped smiling.

"And you know that box of chocolates Auntie Jane sent you? Well, I want you to take it round to Mrs Watson, to say sorry for the rabbit eating her cabbages."

"Oh no, do I have to, Dad . . ."

Benny stood outside Mrs Watson's
door. He was scared. After all, she was a
witch . . .

But when Benny gave her the
chocolates, she was not cross or
witch-like at all.

She was so pleased with the present,
she asked him in.

And she didn't mind about the
cabbages one little bit!

Benny sat by the fire. Mrs Watson gave
him some lemonade.

Benny told her all about Snowy, and
how the birthday cake was ruined.

After lunch, Dad sent Benny into the garden to clean out the rabbit hutch.

"Phew! What a pong!" said Benny to himself, as he swept out all the bits.

Then, as he scrubbed, he smelled a different smell — a delicious smell — and it was coming from Mrs Watson's kitchen.

"Oh, Snowy! It's all your fault. If you hadn't got in the way, I'd still have a birthday cake. And I do *love* icing . . ." sighed Benny.

Poor Snowy, sitting in a basket with the lid shut-tight, just went on nibbling his carrot.

Dad came out to inspect the hutch.

"Well done, Benny. Now come and see what's in the kitchen!"

It was a NEW birthday cake!

Mrs Watson had baked him a huge cake
with white icing and "Happy Birthday
Benny" on it.

"Yummy!" said Benny.

When Benny took Snowy back to
school after half-term, Miss Bell asked
him if everything had been all right.

"Perhaps you would like to look after
him over the Easter holidays, too," said
Miss Bell.

"Well, er, um," said Benny.

"I will have to ask my Dad about
that. . ."